MY AMERICAN JOURNEY

From Slavery to Freedom

with Harriet Tubman

BY DEBORAH HEDSTROM-PAGE

ILLUSTRATIONS BY SERGIO MARTINEZ

Foreword

The Underground Railroad was not a "real" railroad with steam engines and boxcars. It was a maze of night trails, hidden cellars, secret papers, and mysterious signals. It turned pieces of property back into men and women. It brought hope to a sad part of American history. In *From Slavery to Freedom* you'll read about this railroad and about Harriet Tubman, one of the people who made it run.

Slavery is hard to imagine today. We go to the store to buy music CDs, food, clothes, and toys. But 150 years ago, people also went to the market to buy people—people who worked without wages as slaves. Some of these slaves lived pretty good lives with plenty of food and clothing. Others suffered with too little food, too much hard work, and poor places to live. But no matter if their lives were good or bad, they all lacked one thing—freedom.

Many people accepted slavery as a fact of life, but some did not. They knew it was wrong to treat a person as if he or she were a piece of property. So they hid runaway slaves, fed them, gave them money, and did all they could to help them reach freedom. Some of these "railroad agents" were famous people in our history: Allan Pinkerton, Ralph Waldo Emerson, and Susan B. Anthony, to name a few. But most of them were just ordinary people like you or me. They came from different nationalities and had different beliefs and social positions. You're going to meet many of them in this book, especially a brave former slave named Harriet Tubman.

As in all *My American Journey* books, you'll also meet a fictional person. Joshua Whitaker is a Quaker who says "thee" and "thou" instead of "you." And like others who share his faith, he is active in the Underground Railroad. While Joshua himself is fictional, most of the adventures he has in this story happened; they were actually done by real but unknown people. At no time does he change what really happened in history; each escape, each near-capture, and each adventure is true. So gather your courage, wipe your sweaty hands on your pant legs, and get set to knock on another exciting door in American history.

Introduction

Joshua straightened his coat, hoping he looked all of his fourteen years. He knocked on the door of the hotel room—and then suddenly remembered his hat. Quickly he whipped it off his head just as the door opened. A slight, balding man with a rim of dark hair looked at Joshua through wire-framed spectacles. "Yes, how may I help you?"

All of Joshua's well-rehearsed words turned into a mush of thoughts as he faced the famous journalist and antislavery leader. Seconds ticked by. He had to say something! "Mr. Garrison . . . Sir . . . My name is Joshua Whitaker. I want to help thee."

William Lloyd Garrison looked at the boy's plain, dark coat and wide-brimmed hat and knew he was a Quaker. Since coming to Philadelphia to speak to the Pennsylvania Abolition Society, he'd seen many men and boys dressed the same way. "Come in and tell me what you have in mind."

Once seated, Joshua decided to jump right in before his jumbled thoughts disappeared. "All my life my parents taught me that God sees people the same, so I never agreed with slavery. But last month I traveled with my father to Cambridge, Maryland, to buy a prize bull. Outside a tavern, I saw slaves being sold to a trader from the South."

Joshua's fingers crunched the brim of his hat, and he took a breath before continuing. "I'll never forget the boy I saw. He was about my age. A buyer was feeling his muscles and checking his teeth. When the man said he'd take the boy, a black woman off to the side started crying something terrible! I knew she was his mother. The boy tried to look brave, but I saw his eyes. I saw his terror. Right then, I would have given anything to free them. That is why I came to thee."

There was no denying the lad's sincerity, but Mr. Garrison leaned forward and asked, "What of your parents?"

"My father saw the auction too," Joshua answered. "My mother gives food and clothes to those on the Underground Railroad. Both know I am here."

Garrison nodded his bald head and leaned back in the hotel chair. "Let me tell you what joining the

Underground means. If you still feel the same way when I'm done, I'll give you a job.

"More than forty years ago Congress made it illegal to bring slaves from Africa to America, but even so, over three million slaves already live in our country. For years I've spoken and written against slavery. But the truth is, for every American who feels as you and I do, there is one who feels it's right to own slaves and three others who'd rather let well enough alone."

Stopping for a moment, Mr. Garrison got up and walked over to his traveling bag. He took a piece of paper from it, unrolled it, and held it up.

Joshua looked at the poster and dropped his hat. He didn't even pick it up. He just kept reading the bold print in front of him.

Garrison let him finish and then continued, "As you can see by this $5000 reward the state of Georgia has offered for my arrest, those who favor slavery are just as sincere as we are. I've been fined, imprisoned, nearly lynched, and frequently threatened with assassination. And I am not alone. Other abolitionists have risked their homes, their savings, and even their lives. Many are constantly watched, and their mail is even opened and read.

"Do not be fooled by what you see in Philadelphia, Joshua. Unlike other places, your city has favored abolishing slavery since the 1700s. Men like Dr. Benjamin Rush, who provided medical supplies for the Lewis and Clark expedition, and the marquis de Lafayette, who fought in the Revolution, and Ben Franklin, who helped form your good city, are just a few who have stood against slavery in Pennsylvania.

"But the Underground Railroad, or Liberty Line as some call it, reaches far beyond your state's borders. That's why no single person knows everyone who works on the Railroad or even when it was started. Secrecy is what keeps it safe. To be a part of it requires silence as well as courage."

Mr. Garrison paused to let his words sink in. Once again Joshua's mind pictured the son and mother separated at the slave auction. *What if that had been me, and my mother was the one crying?* Slavery needed to be stopped, and he needed to help.

"Mr. Garrison, I will keep silent, and I believe God will give me the courage I need."

"Do you read and write well?" the older man asked.

When Joshua nodded yes, William Lloyd Garrison turned and sat down at the desk. For the next few minutes, only the scratching of a quill pen could be heard. He carefully waited to let the ink dry, then folded the paper he'd written on and handed it to Joshua. "This letter will introduce you

to William Still. He is the secretary of your town's abolition society and one of the leaders in the Underground Railroad. Many runaways stop at his home for food, clothes, and money. He also keeps records so that escaped slaves can find other family members in the North.

"I want you to help him with the recordkeeping. He is a free black, but outside Philadelphia he runs the risk of slave hunters overlooking that fact. Your youth and skin color will allow you to travel without much suspicion or risk. However, you will have to give up your Quaker speech and clothes most of the time. Though not all members of your faith are abolitionists, none would believe a Quaker supported slavery."

Joshua put the letter in his coat pocket and followed his host toward the door. Before he walked out, Mr. Garrison put his hand on Joshua's shoulder and said, "I believe that one day our great country will rid itself of slavery. When it does, all of us will need to remember the importance of putting what is *right* above what is *accepted*. We'll also need to see that the desire for freedom is not limited by race, religion, or where you live."

PHILADELPHIA, PENNSYLVANIA
OCTOBER 1849

Chapter One
OFF THE AUCTION BLOCK

June 1850

After months of taking messages and delivering food and clothes, I finally got to help rescue my first runaways. In the process, I even got shot at!

It all started when I met an escaped slave at the Vigilance Committee office where Mr. Still is secretary. I couldn't help noticing the woman because she came to the place as often as I did. She wore a bright bandanna over her hair and had a big scar on her forehead. Once I saw that she also had whip scars on her neck. She always asked someone to help her check the most recent list of escaped slaves. Then, time after time, she'd walk away with her shoulders sagging. Finally I said in my new practiced speech, "I've seen you here a lot. Are you looking for your family?"

When she heard my voice, she didn't jump like new runaways do. "You can always tell the new runaways," one Railroad agent told me, "'cause they're ready to bolt at the sound of a door shutting, stairs creaking, or even people speaking too loud. It comes from weeks of listening and fearing they'll hear the pounding of horses' hooves, the braying of hounds, or the snap of a stepped-on twig."

Even though the woman wasn't a runaway, she looked me over carefully before answering my question about her family. "Yes, I keep prayin' that my brothers and sisters will make it North."

I liked the sound of her quiet, husky voice and wanted to hear more. "Are they a long way from Philadelphia?"

"Some has been sold south, and I don't know about them. But the others and my parents still live on the plantation in Bucktown, Maryland. It takes three weeks of walking at night to get there."

After that day, the ex-slave woman and I always talked when we saw each other. I learned she worked as a cook in a Philadelphia hotel and that her name was Harriet Tubman.

One time I asked her what freedom felt like after being born a slave. She held up her hands and said, "When I crossed into the free state of Pennsylvania, I looked at my hands to see if I was the same person. There was such a glory over everythin', I felt like I was in heaven."

Though her face lit up as she told of her feelings, I knew living here wasn't easy. Once she told me, "I am a stranger in a strange land, for my home, after all, is down in the old cabin with my old ma and pa and my brothers and sisters. If only they were free."

Our talk was interrupted when an urgent note arrived. An Underground Railroad agent in Cambridge, Maryland, wrote of shipping "two large and two small bales of wool" North. Since slavers watched the agent and read his mail, Mr. Still knew the "bales" had heads, arms, and legs. Mr. Still called me over. "Joshua, isn't your father going to Cambridge again to pick up some more stock?" he asked while refolding the note.

When I nodded he continued, "I want you to go with him and help the local agent in any way you can. A freeman's slave wife and two children are about to be sold south. They're going on the auction block in just a few days."

Next Mr. Still turned to Harriet, "A freeman named John Bowley needs help coming North.

We've got people taking him and his family as far as Baltimore, but we must find an agent to help them further North. Do you remember what agents in that area aided you?"

At the mention of Bowley's name, Harriet gasped. "Oh, Lord! John is my brother-in-law. The master must be sellin' my sister and her children." Even as she spoke, she was turning toward the door. "I'm goin' south to lead them out of Baltimore."

No matter how terrifying Mr. Still made his descriptions of slave hunters, recapture, and punishment, nothing changed Harriet's mind. So while Harriet rode in a hay wagon to Baltimore, I rode in my father's buggy to Cambridge.

Leaving my father to purchase the stock alone, I walked to the agent's house. From the look on John Bowley's face when I arrived, I knew something was wrong. "My wife and children have been on the auction block all morning," John said. "No one has bought them yet, but after lunch they go back out again. Right now they're in the slave pens."

John, the agent, and I talked together, and only one risky plan seemed possible. I wrote a note and handed it to John. He looked scared as he headed out the door. Then the agent and I fidgeted in our seats and tried to make small talk while we waited. It seemed like forever before we heard the door rattle.

I don't mind telling you, I breathed a mighty big sigh of relief when a little girl's head appeared in the door followed by her mother, a baby, and John.

Not taking time for greetings, the agent hustled them off to a trapdoor leading to a small, hidden room behind the cellar. Later I took them some food, and John told me what happened.

"All the way down the street I kept tellin' myself that I couldn't look scared, but when I held out my hand, it was a-tremblin'. Then I hit on the idea of being like an actor in a play. I pulled my head up straight but kept my eyes lowered just like I'd seen house servants do. By the time I reached the auctioneer, I could hand him your note without tremblin'. I said what I'd heard other slaves tell him: 'De master wants me to fetch Mary and her chil'ens up to de hotel. He's done found a buyer for 'em.' "

Though his playacting was over, John's voice still wobbled a little as he continued. "Glancin' past the auctioneer, I looked at Mary. She was frightened, but I could tell she understood that I wanted the man to think I was one of her master's slaves.

"He fell for it. The auctioneer hustled out Mary and the children, telling me to take them up to the hotel right quick," John said as he took a deep breath in relief.

At dusk the family slipped out of the secret second cellar. I took a fishing pole and followed them down to the Choptank River, where a boat with food and blankets waited. The agent told me to row them upriver while they stayed low under a tarp. I was rowing smooth when suddenly an explosive bang shattered the silence, and a bullet whined past my ear!

"Hold off!" I yelled, just before the fright of being shot at sucked all the air out of me.

During the endless seconds that it took for me to catch a breath, some men crashed through the bushes and appeared on shore. One said, "Reily, I told you to wait before firing. That's no runaway; that's a kid doing some night fishing."

"Sorry about that, youngster," he yelled at me. "We're chasing a family of runaways. You seen any on the river?"

"None has come by my boat," I answered sort of truthfully.

Near dawn I spotted my father's buggy waiting on the shore. He told us where to hide the boat and gave John directions to another agent's farm where he and his family could hide through the day.

On the trip home, I dozed off as my father turned onto the road to Philadelphia. My last waking thoughts were: *Will they get to Baltimore and will Harriet be waiting?*

Chapter Two
ESCAPE TO FREEDOM

December 1850

Even six months later, I get knots in my stomach when I think about John and his family's escape. Everything from the whizzing bullet to our scary news sets a person on edge.

When my father and I got back from Cambridge, I headed straight for William Still's home. Maybe he'd heard something about Harriet and John. As I walked, my mind wrestled with questions. What if the slave catchers had found John and his family? What if Harriet had fallen asleep and gotten caught?

My worries made it impossible for me to sit down, and Mr. Still found me pacing in his parlor. "Have you heard anything?" I blurted out.

"At last word, Harriet had reached Baltimore," he said. "A few days later her sister and family made it there too."

It didn't take a lot of imagination to picture the family reunion of hugs, tears, and questions. But they weren't safe yet. "Will they make it?" I asked.

"They must travel many dangerous miles," he answered. "Anyone who sees the group of them will know they are runaways. Since the Nat Turner rebellion in Virginia in 1831, slaves aren't allowed on the roads in groups."

This wasn't what I wanted to hear. Seeing my concern, Mr. Still said, "Come, Joshua, have a glass of lemonade."

The cold, sour-sweet tang of the drink tasted good. Looking up at Mr. Still, my thoughts went from Harriet to the successful coal merchant sitting in front of me. How could he be the child of an escaped slave? He wore a pressed blue suit, starched white shirt, and carefully arranged necktie, yet people said he came to Philadelphia with only five dollars. They also said he taught himself to read and write when he was twenty-three years old. *You'd never guess it now!* I thought as I finished my drink.

A few days later I saw Mr. Still again at the Vigilance Committee office. Right off I knew something was wrong. My stomach twisted up. "Is Harriet safe, sir?" I asked.

"I don't know, but if she makes it, she can't stay here much longer," he said. "The new Fugitive Slave Law has people scared. It says that runaways found anywhere in the United States must be returned to their masters. It also has harsher fines and imprisonment for people who help them."

Mr. Still went over and picked up the written records of runaways and their locations. "We must hide these right away," he said. "Under the new law, authorities can search our homes and businesses. Since I'm a known abolitionist I'll be watched, so we must choose our hiding place with care. We also need to stop runaways from openly coming to this office."

Before I could respond, the outside stairs creaked. I looked toward the door just as it swung open. Harriet and her family had made it!

Though the topic of the new law got lost in the greetings and recordkeeping, Harriet somehow knew things weren't right. After seeing her family settled in my father's barn, she cornered Mr. Still. "I felt fear at the homes where we stopped on the way North," she said. "I felt it again when we got here. What's wrong?"

Mr. Still explained about the new law and ended by saying, "You're no longer safe here. Recaptured slaves can be shot or whipped and sold back to the deep south."

The news didn't seem to upset Harriet. I asked her, "What are you going to do?"

Without any hesitation she turned to me and answered, "Keep working and saving money. Then I will return south for more members of my family."

I couldn't believe it. "Harriet, no! You will be caught or worse still, killed!"

"Maybe so," she said, "but it's fearful headin' out when you've never been far from the plantation and all you know is the North Star. And though the slaves hear whispers about an Underground Railway, they don't know what it is. Back on the plantation, I thought it was a tunnel that went under the ground."

As she spoke of the past, Harriet got a distant look in her eyes, and I realized I was finally going to hear of her escape. She continued, "When word came that I was gonna be sold south, I knew I had to escape. I tried to get my brothers to go with me, but they said, 'We don't know where to go. Master will follow and catch us for sure.'

"But I still had to try, and I thought of a white woman who might help me. She'd come by a field I was workin' in and stopped her wagon beside me.

'How did you get that awful gash on your head?' she asked.

"I told her about the corn shuckin'. I was just a girl, but I was working with the other slaves, including a man we called Ol' Jim. While we was ripping the husks off the corn, I saw the look in Ol' Jim's eyes that day. I knew he was fixin' to take out and try to escape. But the master seen him leave and picked up a piece of iron. I dashed to warn Jim and got in the way of the master's throw. The iron hit me.

"When the woman heard my story, she shook her head and said, 'If you ever need help, see me.'

"So the first night I ran away, I stopped by her house. She hid me and then drove me North under a load of vegetables. She told me of other places to stop. I walked by night, never knowin' if I'd fall into one of my sleeps. Sometimes they just come over me, and before I know it, I'm fast asleep, lying wherever I fall.

"As I went North I hid by day, sleepin' on the ground, in haystacks, and in attics. One farmer put me in a potato hole! I shivered in the cramped place, partly in cold and partly in fear of the blackness around me. But when slave catchers came by the farm, they never checked the little hole."

In my mind I could see Harriet huddled in with the dirt-covered potatoes, mice, spiders, and beetles. I cringed. "Weren't you afraid?"

She nodded but said, "I'd reasoned it out in my mind. I had a right to one of two things, liberty or death. If I couldn't have one, I'd have the other. So I just kept a-prayin', 'Lord, I'm gonna hold steady onto You.' "

Amazed by her story, I asked, "After all that, how can you return to the South?"

My question snapped Harriet out of her past memories. "The good Lord's kept me safe two times, and He knows my family needs me to lead them North."

"But you can't even go to your old cabin," I said.

Harriet smiled. "No need. Folks there know my voice. I'll sing from nearby."

Turning toward the door, she started singing in a rich, low voice.

> *When that old chariot comes,*
> *I'm going to leave you,*
> *I'm bound for the promised land,*
> *Friends, I'm going to leave you.*
> *I'll meet you in the morning,*
> *When I reach the promised land;*
> *On the other side of Jordan,*
> *For I'm bound for the promised land.*

Chapter Three
NO TURNING BACK

January 1852

Every time I dig the record book out of its hiding place in the cemetery, it's a big risk. If it ever got into the wrong hands, hundreds of runaways could be tracked down. But I just had to write about this. It's so unbelievable. How could Harriet take *eleven* slaves to Canada?

It's been more than a year since she left the Vigilance Committee office singing, and she's done what she said she would do. Every five or six months, she goes south and brings us a load of "passengers," as she calls them.

Up until now, the Fugitive Law hasn't been enforced by local authorities. But recently we've heard about Shadrach and Thomas Sims. Shadrach was arrested as a runaway in Boston. Abolitionists broke him out and got him North, but it shook us up, especially Harriet. She'd always thought of Boston as safe. Her last hope for the city died when Thomas was arrested there a few months later. He

was whipped, imprisoned, and then sold and resold in Savannah, Charleston, and New Orleans.

Soon afterward, she told me she was moving across the river to New Jersey. "I gotta be safe while I earn money to take my passengers North."

While Harriet found work as a hotel cook, we also took action because of the Fugitive Law's enforcement. William Still set up the hiding place for our records in the cemetery. Runaways no longer came to the Vigilance office. Instead, at all hours of the night they came to Mr. Still's home, where they received food, clothes, and money.

More than once Mr. Still asked me to take a group and hide them in my father's barn. My parents always greeted these frightened guests with blankets and warm food. One night I asked my father why he kept risking everything he'd worked so hard for. He told me, "All the milk cows in the world aren't worth one human soul."

So we kept on doing what we could. But then I got a note from Mr. Still. It said, "I found Exodus 14 good reading today."

Since I knew the authorities watched our leader, I figured his note meant more than the suggested Bible reading. I turned to the passage and read about Moses being trapped with the Israelites at the Red Sea. The words *Moses* and *trapped* made my heart start pounding. Harriet was in trouble!

Things had changed a few months back when Harriet had gone south to bring her freeman husband North. When she found him, he refused to come—and then he introduced her to his new wife!

This painful experience led to a new desire. She wanted to start rescuing more than family members. She told me, "I work hard at my hotel jobs, but it ain't nothin' like the work in the fields. And anytime I want to quit and get another job, I can. My people won't never know that kind of freedom unless I help them. The strong ones need to be told the way, and the fearful need to be shown the way. Maryland is the land of Egypt, and my people need a Moses to lead them out of there."

From then on, when she arrived in an area, she'd sing the forbidden song, "Let My People Go." Her husky voice would start the slaves whispering, "Moses is here."

Because of Harriet's new name, "Moses," I understood the hidden Bible message and headed straight for Mr. Still's house. When I arrived, he said, "Harriet is coming North with eleven passengers."

Eleven! I couldn't believe it. That many runaways couldn't be easily missed or hidden. Though Mr. Still registered my startled look, he continued, "They're near starving because more than one frightened Underground station has turned away the large group. But that's not all. Harriet must take them on to Canada, and she doesn't know the way."

She'd done it this time! The fear I often felt for her didn't just twist up my insides; now it turned them into huge knots. "What can I do?" I asked.

"Take your father's hay wagon and go meet them outside the city," Mr. Still answered. "At last word from Thomas Garrett they were in bad shape. He sent them on as far as he could in carriages. Now they need us."

That night I drove out of town. The darkness made it useless to watch, so I listened over the rumble of the wagon wheels. Then I heard a voice say, "A friend with friends needs a ride."

At the Underground Railroad password, I halted the horse, and eleven dark bodies climbed into the load of hay. Later, in my parents' barn, I had a chance to really see the people. All wore new shoes, thanks to Mr. Garrett, but they limped. They must have walked barefoot for miles over the frozen ground. Only the baby, drugged into sleeping so it wouldn't cry, did not look frightened. Then I noticed a boy who seemed about my age. With hay still clinging to his clothes and hair, he finished the last of my mother's stew and looked up.

I smiled, sat down, and introduced myself. He told me his name was Lewis. As we talked, I learned about the escape. He said, "As more and more of us gathered in the woods in answer to Moses' singing, I could tell she was gettin' worried. But she wouldn't send anyone back. So we all came together. When we weren't marching at night, we would hole up somewhere. Often we hid and shivered under bushes without food since many homes turned us away, saying, 'Too many. Go someplace else.'

"Finally one of the men said. 'This is worse than being a slave. I'm goin' back to the master's warm cabin.'

"None of us expected what happened next. Moses took out a pistol and pointed it at the man's chest. 'Ain't no one turnin' back. Go on or die,' she told him."

I knew about Harriet's six-shooter. I'd seen it once by accident. When I gasped, she said, "I hate it,

but no one can turn back. The master would force them to tell about the Underground Railroad, bringing grief to all those who help us."

Brushing a bit of hay from his pants, Lewis continued his story. "The man came on with us, headin' North again. The rest of the way Moses told us stories of others who had made it to freedom and of slave ships from long ago. We would have given up if it wasn't for her."

Much later Lewis and I went to sleep. The next day Mr. Still came with clothes and money. I gave my new friend a pair of my black pants. Without their dirty, ragged clothes, the runaways looked like free blacks—except for the fear that remained in most of their eyes. My father and I hoped it didn't show as we drove them out of town at dusk.

We took them to the outskirts of Burlington, New Jersey, and I hated saying good-bye to Lewis. At a different time, in a freer place, we would have been good friends.

Heading home, I thought about Lewis and Harriet. Lewis faced an unknown future, and Harriet had just "stolen" $11,000 worth of "property" from the slaveowner. Thank goodness Reverend Loguen, Frederick Douglass, Henry Thoreau, Susan Anthony, and other Northern agents would help them now. But would they make it safely to Canada?

Chapter Four
A CHRISTMAS ESCAPE

December 1854

Lately my spirit's been feelin' heavy for my brothers. I know danger is comin' on them. Will you write a message for me to Ol' Jacob Jackson?" Harriet asked me one day. "He's a friend livin' near my folk."

One look at her troubled face and I said yes even though I wanted to say no. I knew the letter would probably cause her to head into danger again. She'd been working as a cook and saving money, which meant she was planning another rescue trip.

"Harriet, you can't keep doing this," I said. "You did the impossible by getting those eleven runaways to Saint Catherines in Canada. Since then you've made a couple of trips each year to bring slaves North. You will get caught sooner or later. Didn't you hear about Anthony Burns in Boston?"

I knew she'd heard. Everybody had heard. Just a few months earlier, President Pierce had sent a whole detachment of marines and artillery to stand against the citizens of Boston who had tried to keep Burns, a runaway, from being returned to his owner. The government had started enforcing the Fugitive Slave Law, and Harriet could become their next target. And besides that, there was a reward on her head, though the posters identified her only as "Moses."

Without answering my question about Burns, Harriet straightened and faced me. She couldn't look me straight in the eyes anymore because I'd grown a few inches in the last couple of years, but it didn't matter. She had a way of seeming ten feet tall. She told me, "I've been dreamin' about my brothers gettin' sold and goin' on a chain gang. I know the good Lord's warnin' me that they need my help."

How could I argue? I went and got paper and ink. "What do you want me to write?" I asked.

She answered, "I know the letter will be read by officials, seein' how it's goin' to Jacob, a free

black, and comin' from the North. We got to make it say somethin' without seemin' to."

In the end I wrote the letter pretending to be Jacob's son who lived in New York. After mentioning the weather and such, Harriet had me add, "Read my letter to the old folks and give my love to them. And tell my brothers to be always watching unto prayer, and when the good old ship of Zion comes along, to be ready to step on board."

Later, we learned the letter caused some trouble. Jacob's folks were dead, and he only had one son. The inspectors called him in to ask about the letter. They read it to him, and he shook his head. "That letter can't be meant for me; I can't make heads or tails of it."

But Jacob did know what it meant. By evening, he'd told Harriet's brothers that judging by the date of the letter, she would be coming for them around Christmas.

Icicles hung from the eaves on the morning Harriet went south. Once when I'd asked her why she traveled in winter, she'd said it was because of Christmas. "It's the only time that slaves don't work. As long as the Yule log burns, they can stay in the cabins. If I time it right, the masters don't know the slaves are gone for two days."

Harriet made the most of those two days to get the slaves far away from their masters. Once the slave catchers and their dogs took out, she and her passengers would have to hole up for days. When she had brought out the eleven, it had taken three weeks to get out of Maryland and then only one more week to go all the way to Canada. That's because once in the North, the runaways could ride trains, boats, or buggies as long as they changed clothes and had money.

Writing all this down doesn't make the waiting any easier. While I milk the cows, run messages, and read Mrs. Stowe's book *Uncle Tom's Cabin*, Harriet sings behind the slave quarters, crosses frozen streams, and hides in haystacks. But finally one night when I was at Mr. Still's, we heard a knock and the familiar words, "A friend with friends."

It was Harriet! She and her three brothers and four others stood in the doorway. Mr. Still went to get some hot soup while I got the cold runaways some blankets and led them to the fire. That's when I noticed that Harriet had walked her shoes off!

Later I got to talking with her brother, Benjamin. He told me some of what happened. He said, "Never did a song ever make my heart jump so high as when I heard Ol' Hat singin'—that's what we call Harriet. She was singin', 'Tell old Pharaoh, "Let my people go."' Me, William, and John were gonna be sold to a chain gang when the Yule Log burned out.

"But we didn't get away as fast as Hat hoped, because John's missis was havin' her first young'n'. It was real hard leavin' her behind with their tiny, new son. And we all hated to leave our old ma and pa too. But finally we came along 'cause we knew if we didn't go North, we'd soon be clanking in chains down south.

"Waitin' for the baby to come gave us a late start and forced us to hide out in a barn until it was safe to move on. All of us got mighty hungry, and finally Hat sent one of the other slaves to get some food from our pa."

"But why didn't Harriet go herself so she'd see her folks at Christmas?" I asked.

"Oh, she wanted to more than anythin'," he told me. "But Ol' Rit—that's our ma—is given to cryin' and carryin' on when she gets excited. The ruckus could of given us away. And Pa Ben is known to never tell a lie. The slave we sent for food told him we were there, and Pa Ben brought the stuff to us hisself. But he put a blindfold on so that when the master asked him if he'd seen us, he could truthfully answer, 'No sir.'"

Benjamin, Harriet, and the others left for Canada in the morning. She says it's easier to cross out of the United States now because there's a new suspension bridge at Niagara Falls. She and the others should make it to safety, then Harriet will be back.

I saw her noticing her brother John's sadness. I know her mind is already planning how to get his wife and baby son North. I understand. I want to get them to John too. But how many times can Harriet keep going back and not get caught?

Chapter Five
ALMOST CAPTURED!

November 1856

Harriet's really done it this time! She'll get caught for sure because of the new runaway poster that's going up everywhere. It's different from the other ones we see tacked on buildings, trees, and signposts. Most of them show a black figure with a sack on a stick over his shoulder with descriptions printed below. But the new one has something else:

A big reward, $2,600, and Josiah isn't going to be hard to miss, being tall and well built with that scar on his face. His back even has unhealed whip marks all over it. But that didn't stop Harriet. She's the one taking Josiah and two other runaways North!

When word came through the Underground that our Harriet was leading this marked man, even Mr. Still lost his usual calm. He took a big gulp of hot tea, pausing to let the burning liquid take the edge off the news. Then he shook his head and said, "Oh, Harriet, you've done yourself in this time."

I tried doing chores to keep busy, but I couldn't keep my mind off the danger Harriet was in. Finally I just had to do something. I told Mr. Still, "I've got to go out and help her. I know most of the places she stops."

Mr. Still agreed and the next day I drove my father's wagon to Wilmington, Delaware.

Once in town, I left my wagon at a public stable before quietly walking to Thomas Garrett's home. I didn't want to advertise my going to this man since he was a well-known abolitionist. As a matter of fact, a few years earlier a court had fined him $5,400 for helping a freeman get his enslaved family to safety. He answered the judge by saying, "I have always been fearful of losing what I own. But now that you have relieved me, I will go home and put another story on my house, so that I can accommodate more of God's poor."

When I met the man who'd spoken so boldly, he surprised me. I knew he shared my Quaker faith and was a successful businessman, but I'd expected him to be younger. It amazed me that this white-haired man risked so much. Once again I realized the Underground Railroad knew no limits in age, wealth, or religion. I'd seen wealthy businessmen and poor farmers provide hiding places. And although many of us Quakers took part in the Freedom Line, I'd also met Roman Catholics, Protestants, and Jews.

But in spite of these people's devotion to ending slavery, I knew Mr. Garrett was right when he said, "Fear will keep many agents from helping this marked Josiah Bailey and those with him. Your friend Harriet will be desperate if she gets them this far."

Hearing this, I felt helpless and thought, What can I do?

As if in answer to my unspoken question, Mr. Garrett said, "Some friendly bricklayers need a strong back and an extra wagon. Go there and work for them, and every evening take your wagon of bricks out past the town patrols. Look and listen for a while. Perhaps you'll hear a friend whisper."

The next day I laid brick and then toward evening rode out of town with one of the other bricklayers. Once past the last bridge, we stopped and waited. A short while later we heard the familiar words, "A friend with friends."

The voice was so hoarse, I didn't know for sure it was Harriet's until she stepped out from some bushes. One look told me she was sick, but then my attention turned to the other woman and two men who stood up. Seeing a tall, well-built black man with a face scar, I didn't need to be told which one was Josiah—and neither would anyone else who'd seen his runaway poster! How on earth would we get them past the bridge patrol?

To my amazement, the bricklayer was taking the bricks out of the wagon. We all helped and soon had it empty. Then the man told everyone to climb into the wagon and lie flat. Putting a board over them, he had me help him stack the bricks on top. After only a few bricks, I heard the slave woman let out a low gasp of terror. We stopped, but then we heard Harriet's hoarse voice say gently, "I know it's like a coffin, but we gotta go free or die."

The patrols must have thought no one could possibly be under a load of bricks, because they took one look and waved us past. Behind Mr. Garrett's two-story home, I never unloaded a wagon so fast! When we lifted the board off the gasping, exhausted, and sick fugitives, they headed straight into the house for a little food and a lot of sleep. It wasn't until the next evening that I heard what happened.

Josiah told the story since Harriet still didn't have her voice back. "After I read Harriet one of them posters about me, she knew we'd be follered hard, and started us a-hurryin'. Then all of a sudden she slowed down. The next thing we know, she fell asleep in the middle of the road!"

Seeing the others nod, I couldn't help asking, "What'd you do?"

"Propped her against a tree and waited until she woke up the next day," he said. "As soon as Harriet saw we were in the road, she took off into the bushes, back the way we came. She was saying something about the Lord giving her a vision, but my brother Bill started a-frettin' that she was takin' us back to our master. That's when we come to this big creek—a deep, *freezing* creek."

Hearing Harriet cough, no one needed to tell me that she had waded right in. "That there water came right up to her chin, but with each step she just kept saying. 'The Lord showed me we'll make it. There's a cabin with friendly folks on the other side.'

"We doubted her but kept a-walkin'. Sure enough, we made it across and found a cabin. The next day the man who lived there showed us a way around the stream, and we passed where Harriet had fallen asleep. The ground was trampled with horse and dog tracks, and there was a mess of cigarette stubs lying about. Them slave catchers had lost our tracks at the stream and then must of waited for hours. It surely sent chills up my spine, realizing how Harriet's vision saved our lives!"

Josiah Bailey wasn't the only one with chills streaking up his spine!

Two days later we made it to Philadelphia. Harriet and her passengers couldn't stay long with such a marked man among them. After they left, I told my parents about the trip. Then something I'd been thinking just sort of came out: "Slavery hurts the owner as well as the slave."

My father nodded and let me continue. "Josiah's master offered a big reward because Josiah had run his plantation well for six years as a 'hired' slave; he actually belonged to someone else, but this man paid Josiah's owner to have him work his farm. Finally he was able to buy Josiah from the other man. The morning after the sale, he told his new slave to strip to the waist for a whipping. Surprised, Josiah asked why. His new master said, 'You've been a fine slave. But now you belong to me, and I want you to know it.'

"Josiah ran away right after the beating."

Tall as I was, my father put his arm around my shoulders and said, "You're thinking right, son, but it's a hard thing you've learned."

Chapter Six
GITTY-UP, DOLLIE

July 1857

Harriet's dreams are going to get her killed. At this very moment she's riding a train back to her old master's place in Bucktown, Maryland, in broad daylight, no less! I tried to talk her out of it, but she just kept saying, "I seen it in my dreams. Daddy Ben and Ma Rit are gonna be sold. I gotta get them North."

If only she'd let me go with her! But she says, "I'm a-travelin south. No one looks for runaways goin' in that direction. I'll be plum safe."

I wish I shared her confidence. Harriet's danger grows with each zero added to the reward on her wanted poster. A committee of slaveholders met recently and decided to make an all-out effort to catch the slave stealer called Moses. The rewards on her head now total $40,000! The only good thing is that they still think she's a man.

But the reward is not all; Harriet couldn't have picked a worse time to head south.

Everyone's upset about the Dred Scott court case. After living and marrying in a free state, this runaway slave said he was a United States citizen and therefore free. But the courts said he wasn't a person; he was a piece of property without rights. Even now his master is taking him back to his plantation. The trial might be over, but everyone sure keeps talking about it. And now Harriet is riding right into the thick of it.

But trying to talk her out of going, Mr. Still and I hit a brick wall. No matter what we said, she wouldn't listen. "What if someone recognizes you? Your parents are old; there's no way they can walk all the way North. Besides, you haven't had enough time to save money for this trip."

"The Lord already took care of that, just like the Almighty's gonna take care of me 'til my work for Him is done," she told me.

I didn't see her off at the train station, hoping not to draw any attention to her. I wanted to go to

Mr. Garrett's house in Maryland, but Mr. Still thought all my trips south might begin to arouse suspicion. So I waited, milking cows, chopping wood, running errands, and keeping as busy as I could. As usual, I checked with Mr. Still every day.

One time I got there and found him holding a note and smiling. Seeing me, he chuckled and said, "It's from Frederick Douglass, telling me how Harriet got the money for this trip. She went to a New York businessman and told him she wanted twenty dollars. Shocked, he asked who had told her to come to him. She said, 'The Lord told me.'

"The businessman said the Lord was wrong this time. She shook her head, saying, 'No sir, the Lord's never mistaken! I'm gonna sit here 'til I get it.'"

I could just picture Harriet standing up to the shocked man, and I had to laugh myself. She might not be able to read or write and she might work as a cook and a housemaid, but when it came to "the Lord's work," she'd tackle the king of England!

The letter went on to tell of her falling into one of her sleeps, and when she woke up, she had sixty dollars. As it turned out, she did get the Lord's message a little crossed. The businessman didn't give the money, but those who visited his office and heard about Harriet's request did!

Even as Mr. Still and I shared another good laugh, I couldn't help feeling some relief. With that kind of money, Harriet's chances were better.

Sure enough, a few nights later, Harriet arrived with her parents. Her dad carried a broadax and her mom a feather quilt. None looked the worse for wear, and I was dying to find out how she'd pulled off this latest rescue.

Later that night she told me. "I just took Ol' Dollie right outta the master's pasture and hitched her to an ol' wagon with just a board for sittin'."

I couldn't believe it. "You mean no one saw you?" I asked.

"The old master, Doc Thompson, saw me right after I got off the train, but I'd bought a couple of live chickens just in case. When the master came near me, I jerked the string tied around their legs, and they set to fluttering and squawking, finally getting loose. I hobbled after them like an old lady. The master laughed, sayin', 'Go get 'em, Granny! I'll bet on the chickens, but do it anyway.'"

Harriet also said a slave saw her getting the wagon. "I held my finger to my lips, and he just watched. Never said a word."

Riding in the wagon, Harriet and her folks still hid in the woods by day and traveled by night. They knew they'd be chased since her father was supposed to go to the master's house for questioning the next morning.

Harriet's fear for her parents had been right. Her father told me, "I helped a runaway who later got re-took. He told his master about my help, and every mornin' since then the master's been questioning me. I told him I'd never seen the slave before, and I hadn't. The barn was so dark, I couldn't see nothin'.

"I've never lied to the master, and he knowed it. I'm also a good slave, real faithful. So he didn't sell me right off. But those other masters didn't believe me, and they kept wanting me sold. The way I got called up to the big house every mornin' and asked questions, I knew it was just a matter of time before I'd be on the auction block. Then Hat came a-singin'."

In spite of the telltale wagon tracks and the need to find special hiding places that her older parents could manage, Harriet got her folks to Mr. Garrett's house in Maryland. The clothes he gave them took away their fugitive look. They were wearing the same ones when they left here for Canada.

After they departed, I thought about some of the things Harriet's mother told about her.

She said the scars around her neck and shoulders came from watching a baby. Though only seven years old, the mistress beat Harriet on her neck and shoulders with a strap any time the baby cried.

She went on to say, "After that, Hat got to work in the woods chopping firewood with her pa. She got powerful strong. Why, the master even made her lift heavy loads and such just to show off her muscles to visitin' folks."

Harriet heard her mom talking with me and cut in, "Little did they know, them masters were preparin' me to be Moses. I learned to sleep mighty light, carin' for that babe. No slave catcher gonna rustle a leaf without awakenin' me. And my strength makes it so I can carry a child many a mile."

Harriet's strength and alertness have helped her make trip after trip into the South. And the divine help she seems to get causes even those without any faith to wonder about God. But tension over slavery is tearing at our country. The South wants to keep its slaves, and tempers are short. In such conditions, her danger just keeps growing and growing.

My thoughts make me feel all tight inside.

Chapter Seven
A DETECTIVE HELPS

February 1859

I just got back from Boston. There's so much to write! Our country is tearing itself into two pieces, and outside Pennsylvania I saw the ragged edges even more clearly.

I left home when Mr. Still asked me to go North. He said, "Trouble is brewing. The Kansas-Nebraska Act has turned those territories into a battleground over slavery."

I'd heard about the troublesome law he was describing. Back in 1854, Northern and Southern congressmen were constantly fighting about whether slavery should be allowed in new states coming into the Union. Things got so bad, it became impossible for any new states to join. Then Stephen Douglas came up with the idea of letting each territory's settlers vote to declare themselves either a slave or a free state. The resulting law was named the Kansas-Nebraska Act, because those were the two territories that were waiting for Congress to decide if they could

become states. But as soon as the law was passed, a rush of slaveholders and abolitionists poured into the area.

Arguments and fights resulted, with pro-slavery terrorists attacking abolitionist settlers. That angered a man named John Brown, who sent some of his well-armed sons to protect the abolitionists in the territory. Two years later the first of many deadly battles took place. Things got so bad, many people started calling that area "Bleeding Kansas."

Mr. Still told me, "To help the abolitionists' cause, Frederick Douglass and others in New York urged Harriet to lecture in and around Boston. She felt unsure at first. But she needed money for more rescue trips and for payments on a home she was buying in New York. She bought it for her parents, who couldn't survive Canada's winters."

They weren't the first runaways who wanted to leave Canada. Harriet said many of the former

slaves coming from the warm south suffered from the freezing Northern winters. With little or no money, food and shelter were hard enough to get, let alone coats, shoes, and coal.

"Her lecturing goes well," Mr. Still continued. "But since she can't read and write, I'd like you to join her and keep a record of where she speaks and the names of those who support her. We're going to need more Underground stations as things get worse. Why, I just heard that Stephen Douglas has been debating slavery with another politician named Abraham Lincoln."

After arriving in Boston, I wasn't surprised to discover that Harriet was popular with audiences. Having been spellbound by her stories myself, I knew the power of her words. Somehow she made the listeners feel like they were the ones ducking into bramble bushes, hiding in secret attics, dodging hounds, and sleeping in the wild. Though she sometimes fell into her sleeps on stage, my list of her supporters grew.

Listening to people, I've learned that Harriet has acquired other names besides "Moses" and "Hat."

Folks here in the North call her "Molly Brown" after the woman cannoneer in the Revolution. John Brown refers to her as "General Tubman."

Speaking of Mr. Brown, he caused quite a stir last month. He loaded a wagon with eleven runaways and left Missouri for Canada. Harriet and I, traveling with abolitionists, met one of the women who helped them on the last leg of their thousand-mile wintertime journey.

The woman had talked with a couple of the runaways and learned about an agent named Allan Pinkerton who had helped them in Chicago. He's a detective! Since the only detective I'd ever heard of was one Edgar Allan Poe made up in his book *The Murders in the Rue Morgue*, I asked about this real one. She told me, "He's a barrel maker, and he hid the runaways in his factory."

"I thought you said he's a detective," I asked.

"He is, but he was a barrel maker first. He came to Chicago from Scotland about fifteen years ago and opened his factory. A few years later he found out about some counterfeiters and helped capture them. Next thing you know, he was made the county sheriff. He must have liked to figure out crimes, because then he started the Pinkerton National Detective Agency. In 1850, he was appointed Chicago's first detective."

Learning about Mr. Pinkerton made me respect him. He risked this new and exciting career to become an Underground agent. It's good for the Railroad that he did! He not only hid Mr. Brown and his runaways, he got them safely to Detroit, where the lady I met helped them get on a ferry to Canada.

I've not only heard about daring abolitionists since I started traveling with Harriet, I've met a few too! I shook hands with Frederick Douglass and heard him speak. Right off I saw why folks doubted that he was ever a slave. His clear voice, dramatic gestures, and penetrating eyes make him a polished and appealing speaker.

I got a big surprise one night when a man introduced himself as Captain Smith and asked for Harriet. She took one look at him and, knowing him by his real name, said, "Captain Brown!"

I couldn't believe I was looking at the man who'd just traveled a thousand miles with eleven runaways. In the days that followed, he questioned Harriet about Maryland. She drew crude maps, showing him good hiding places and escape routes out of the state. Right before I had to return home to help on the farm, I heard him ask her to encourage runaways to join his band of men.

Riding home on the train, my mind was torn in two directions by Mr. Brown. I did not doubt that he truly cared for Harriet and her people, but his hatred for all who did not oppose slavery bothered me. He was willing to use violence in opposing slavery, and neither Harriet nor I believed that was right. Still, his plan to free the slaves impressed her, and she had agreed to help him.

As the countryside whizzed past my window, I prayed, "Lord, protect Harriet. Don't let her get caught up in this man's hatred."

Chapter Eight
ONE LAST RESCUE

February 28, 1861

The country is breaking in two, and Harriet just stepped into the crack! I guess it was too much to expect that she'd stay up north, lecturing in the cities. John Brown's hanging upset her, but I think Charles Nalle's arrest and rescue is what really triggered her trip back to the South for more slaves.

For a while it looked like Harriet would stay in the North. Everywhere she spoke, folks clapped, cheered, and gave her money to help runaways and to pay for her home in New York. She doesn't need to worry about recapture while she is in the North, because most Northern folks now openly oppose the Fugitive Slave Law. The violence in Kansas and the laws forced on them by the split in Congress left most Northerners angry. Even if runaways do get captured in the North, crowds free them.

John Brown's trial helped rile things up too. He had planned an armed uprising by the slaves that was to begin with a raid on the weapons arsenal at Harpers Ferry, Virginia. Colonel Robert E. Lee led the soldiers who captured Brown and his men. After a fast trial, he was hanged. He died, but his cause did not. While slave owners called him a traitor, abolitionists called him a martyr. Even in the jail that held him, a piece of Southern cotton rope was displayed with a sign that said, "No Northern hemp shall help to punish our felon."

Later Harriet told me she'd waited for word from Captain Brown to come help him. After the hanging, she learned he had sent a number of messages, but they never reached her. When she told me this, I couldn't help thinking back to my prayer.

Though Harriet was kept free from involvement with Brown, his commitment to her people made her question her safe, comfortable role as a lecturer. She told me, "I know why I care about my people, but Captain Brown was a noble and strong white man.

Why should he take upon hisself the burden of despised folk?"

In spite of her question and her growing discontent with the easy life of lecturing, she continued to do it until last spring. But then she heard an angry crowd while waiting for a train to Boston. A fugitive slave had been captured, and the police were trying to drag him into the courthouse against the crowd's wishes.

A man I'd met in Boston wrote and told me, "Harriet took one glance at the situation and went into action. She pulled a couple of young black boys aside and told them to head up the street and yell, 'Fire!' Then she stooped her shoulders and pulled her bonnet down. Looking like an old lady, she made her way up to the runaway slave, a man named Charles Nalle.

"Iron chains hung from his wrists, but Harriet locked her arm through his. At the first cry of 'Fire!' she started pulling Charles through the crowd. The guards struck her, but she didn't stop. As soon as she got the runaway into the mass of people, she took off her bonnet and put it on Charles. A rescue wagon had already been parked down a street, and in no time the two were heading to a safe hiding place."

This rescue turned Harriet's thoughts back to her people in the South. We found this out a few months later when Thomas Garrett wrote to Mr. Still. "Harriet Tubman is again in these parts. She arrived last evening from one of her trips of mercy to God's poor, bringing two men with her. One had a wife and three children, but they were left some thirty miles below. I gave Harriet ten dollars to hire a man with a carriage for them. I shall be uneasy until I hear they are safe."

Mr. Garrett wasn't the only one who was uneasy! The roads are doubly guarded these days, and Negroes rarely get to travel. The South feels certain that all Northerners supported John Brown, and they fear a slave uprising.

Despite this added danger, the next night a familiar knock once again rattled Mr. Still's door while I was there. With a sense of relief, I let in Harriet and her passengers. One look at the man with his wife and two young children clinging to them and the baby in Harriet's arms, and I knew why she'd left Northern safety. Behind the family stood a frightened man and another woman. I looked at Harriet puzzled. She waved a hand, "We picked up that woman along the road after leaving Mr. Garrett."

Seven more free lives. Seven more people no longer treated as if they were pieces of property. Could any of us sacrifice too much for this?

Harriet got these last passengers to Canada right after Abraham Lincoln was elected president. A few weeks later, South Carolina announced it was leaving the United States. Even as I write this, more Southern states are leaving the Union and forming the Confederate States of America. President Lincoln has made it clear that the country will not be split apart without a fight.

As Quakers, my parents and I do not hold with war and will not fight. But already we've talked of helping all who come to our door. We know that freedom for all people living in the United States will cost many lives.

I don't doubt that Harriet will be in the war. Where her people are, she will be. But it's something else too. Before she left for Canada this last time, she told me that she'd had a dream about all slaves being free. "I've already celebrated their freedom, Joshua. One day soon, you'll see my people walkin' free."

Somehow, some way, I believe Harriet "Moses" Tubman's dream will come true.

November 1870

Ten years ago I buried Mr. Still's record of escaped slaves for safekeeping the last time. Protected by the cemetery's dirt, it lay unused and unread for four years while our country fought its most terrible war—brother against brother, neighbor against neighbor, American against American. But in the end Harriet's dream of freedom for her people did come true.

When President Lincoln declared war on the Confederate States, Northern armies marched south, freeing slaves as they went. The secret, quiet activities of the Underground Railroad burst into the open. Black and white alike joined the Union troops, including Harriet.

Less than a year after her last slave rescue trip into the South, she returned there on the government ship *Atlantic*. She got off at Port Royal, a Union-held island off the South Carolina coast. Escaped slaves had flocked to the island, many suffering from wounds or sickness. She helped Union soldiers who were sick with dysentery, smallpox, and fevers. She wasn't afraid. She said, "The Lord will take care of me 'til my time comes, and then I'll be ready to go."

A year later President Lincoln signed the Emancipation Proclamation, declaring, "all persons held as slaves within any State shall be then, thenceforward and forever free." Shortly afterward Harriet saw her first Union regiment of black soldiers. She later told me, "I felt so proud, and as soon as I could I joined them as a spy and scout."

This daring work came to an end when Confederate General Robert E. Lee surrendered on April 9, 1865. The Union won, and Congress passed the Thirteenth Amendment to the United States Constitution. It made owning slaves a crime.

Harriet and her people played a significant part in this victory. More than two hundred thousand black men became Union soldiers, and almost thirty-eight thousand of them died in battle. Sixteen showed such gallantry that they were given the Medal of Honor by Congress.

Another person who played an important role during the Civil War was Frederick Douglass. He became an adviser to President Lincoln and helped him better understand the plight of slaves. Lincoln believed that slavery was morally wrong, but at first he didn't feel that the problem could be fixed by the government. In time he realized that as long as a major part of the country depended on slaves to earn money, they would not be set free without the government's help.

Allan Pinkerton also helped in the war. During the first year of fighting, he uncovered a plot to assassinate President Lincoln and saved his life. He went on to organize the Secret Service for the federal government but later quit when he got frustrated with all the meddlesome politicians. If only he'd stayed! Perhaps I would not need to write that President Lincoln was killed by an assassin's bullet right after the war ended.

With the war over, Harriet returned to her home in New York. I visited her there recently. I got a real shock when a man answered my knock on her door. Harriet is married! Her husband is a fine black man who fought in the Civil War. I was sorry to learn, however, that he has tuberculosis.

I also felt sorrow when a former abolitionist friend told me, "Harriet hasn't been paid one cent for her services to the Union Army. Though a group of us petitioned that she be granted a pension, it was denied. As a result, she almost lost her home, but then a wonderful woman named Sarah Bradford wrote Harriet's biography. She called the book *Scenes in the Life of Harriet Tubman,* and it was published in 1869. It has sold well, and Harriet still has her home."

Mr. Still is also writing a book about the Underground Railroad. Digging up the old records and rereading them has brought back a lot of memories. So many events have happened since I gathered my courage and knocked on the hotel door of William Lloyd Garrison. So many changes have taken place since I noticed a black woman with a bandanna and a scar at the Vigilance Committee office. But I think the party tonight will somehow tie them all together.

William Still's family is celebrating "Still Day," and many who escaped on the Underground Railroad will be at the party. But they won't be runaways. They'll be United States citizens with the right to vote, thanks to the Fourteenth and Fifteenth Amendments.

As these citizens get together tonight, they'll remember close calls with slave catchers, special people who opened their homes to ragged fugitives, first jobs with paychecks, and Civil War battles. They'll talk of abolition leaders such as Thomas Garrett, Sojourner Truth, Frederick Douglass, and "Moses" Tubman. And for old time's sake, they may sing a song; perhaps the one Josiah Bailey sang when he crossed the Canadian border to freedom:

Go down, Moses,
Way down in Egypt's land.
Tell old Pharaoh,
Let my people go!

Faith

Character Building with Harriet Tubman

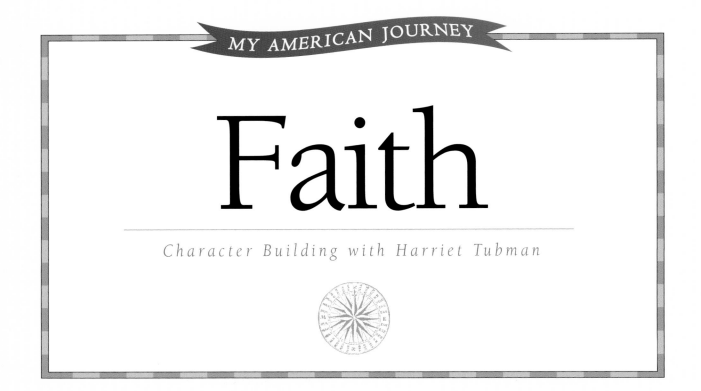

Faith:

A Step Beyond What We Can Figure Out

Understanding faith can be tough because it often involves believing in things that a person can't see, taste, smell, hear, or figure out. But nobody denies that it exists; they use it every day. They believe in their abilities, so they start a new project. They believe in love, so they get married. They believe in God, so they pray.

Ability, love, God, and many other things cannot be figured out by using our senses. It takes faith to include them in our lives, and Harriet Tubman, the woman we just met earlier, had lots of faith. Every time she took slaves out of the South, she had faith in her abilities, in the members of the Underground Railroad, and most of all, in God.

Looking at Harriet Tubman's life will help us understand faith better. Her choices and actions provide a hear/taste/touch example of it. They help us "see" faith. So let's look at her story again and go on a chapter-by-chapter "faith" hunt. Then we'll answer some questions and think about some Bible verses and quotes in order to understand how faith can make a difference in our lives.

CHAPTER ONE

Off the Auction Block

As the flower is before the fruit, so is faith before good works.
ARCHBISHOP WHATELY

1. Write down two things that Harriet did in Philadelphia that showed she had faith. You'll find both on the previous page.

_____

_____

_____

_____

When you have faith about something, you keep checking to see if it has happened. You also do a lot of talking to the One who makes things happen.

2. Harriet's faith eventually took her out of Philadelphia and into danger. Jot down why she left town and where she went.

_____

_____

STUCK? *In 1850 slavery was a vital part of Southern farming. Knowing this, where would be the worst place in the United States for an escaped slave to go?*

W H A T   T H E   B I B L E   S A Y S

Read James 2:14
What good is it, my brothers,
if someone says he has faith, but does not have works?
Can his faith save him?

According to this verse, faith is more than just a feeling that stays inside a person. Think about the words above and then write down what a person's faith will produce.

I T ' S   Y O U R   T U R N

Write down what you thought faith meant before doing this lesson. (I know it's hard, but do your best.)

In addition to the verse above, think about Whately's quote and Harriet's actions. Now rewrite your definition of faith.

CHAPTER TWO

Escape to Freedom

Our faith triumphs o'er our fears.

HENRY WADSWORTH LONGFELLOW

1. Reread where Harriet tells about her own escape to freedom (p. 17). Picture yourself creeping out of a cabin on a dark night to go to a place you don't know. Name three things that would make you feel afraid.

_____

_____

_____

2. Harriet knew that she could die on her way north, but what two things helped her overcome her fears?

_____

_____

STUCK? *One of the things can be copied from the book, but the other one takes some thinking, so consider this: can you overcome a fear by denying it?*

WHAT THE BIBLE SAYS

Read Luke 8:22–25
One day [Jesus] and His disciples got into a boat, and He told them,
"Let's cross over to the other side of the lake."
So they set out, and as they were sailing He fell asleep.
Then a fierce windstorm came down on the lake;
they were being swamped and were in danger.
They came and woke Him up, saying, "Master, Master, we're going to die!"
Then He got up and rebuked the wind and the raging waves.
So they ceased, and there was a calm.
He said to them, "Where is your faith?"

This incident in the Bible tells about a time that the disciples were really afraid. After Jesus got things calmed down, He basically asked them why they lacked faith and feared. How do you think faith can overcome fear?

IT'S YOUR TURN

Write down one thing that you are afraid of: passing a test, not making a sports team . . . .

Now, try what Harriet did:

1. Face your fear: admit you could fail, get hurt, or not make it.
2. Pray about it, knowing that whatever happens, God will somehow use it for good in your life.

No Turning Back

Let us have faith that right makes might,
and in that faith let us to the end dare to do our duty as we understand it.
ABRAHAM LINCOLN

1. Harriet never let any of her "passengers" turn back and return to their old masters. Why?

_____

_____

_____

2. What did she use to back up her words?_____

3. Harriet did more than refuse to let others turn back. She never turned back either, even when leading the runaways looked impossible. Name two things that could have made Harriet return to the South, or even turn back after getting to the North.

_____

_____

STUCK? *Think of numbers and laws.*

WHAT THE BIBLE SAYS

Read 2 Timothy 4:7
I have fought the good fight,
I have finished the race,
I have kept the faith.

According to this verse, what do we need to do to keep faith?

IT'S YOUR TURN

In the last lesson, you wrote down one thing that you were afraid of, and then you faced it and prayed about it.

Now you need to do it.

CHAPTER FOUR

A Christmas Escape

Lord, make me an instrument of Your peace.
Where there is hatred let me sow love;
where there is injury, pardon;
where there is doubt, faith;
where there is despair, hope;
where there is darkness, light;
and where there is sadness, joy.

SAINT FRANCIS OF ASSISI

1. By the time Harriet rescued her brothers, she knew each trip into the South would bring hardships. Write down two hardships mentioned in chapter four.

_____

_____

2. In spite of these hardships, Harriet went south for her brothers. She said she believed the Lord told her something. Write down what she believed He said.

_____

_____

_____

STUCK? *Look on page 22.*

WHAT THE BIBLE SAYS

Read Hebrews 12:2
Keeping our eyes on Jesus, the source and perfecter of our faith,
who for the joy that lay before Him
endured a cross and despised the shame,
and has sat down at the right hand of God's throne.

When it comes to going through hardships because of faith, we have the example of Jesus Christ to follow. What hardships does this verse say that He suffered?

IT'S YOUR TURN

If you have done what you were afraid of, you are either feeling good or feeling bad, depending on how it turned out. If things went well and you're feeling good, thank the Lord for helping you. If things went poorly and you're feeling bad, reread the verse above. Jesus has been where you are and He understands. Talk to Him.

CHAPTER FIVE

Almost Captured!

Things of God that are marvelous
are to be believed on a principle of faith, not to be pried into by reason.
For if reason set them open before our eyes, they would no longer be marvelous.

S. GREGORY

1. In chapter five, two things happen that could have gotten Harriet captured. Write them down.

_____

_____

_____

_____

Before Harriet left the South with her "passengers" on this trip, she knew she'd face two things that could get her captured—one she faced every trip, but the other was new.

2. When things looked their worst, Harriet did something that seemed impossible. Write it down.

_____

_____

STUCK? *Though Harriet couldn't read a map, somehow she knew where to go.*

WHAT THE BIBLE SAYS

Read Hebrews 11:3
*By faith we understand that the universe was created
by the word of God,
so that what is seen has been made from
things that are not visible.*

The world today is pretty skeptical when it comes to miracles. But this verse says that something we see every day came from a miracle. What is it?

IT'S YOUR TURN

We read about miracles in the Bible, but sometimes it's hard to believe in them today. Take a minute and think about Harriet. She didn't have a Bible, and even if she'd had one, she couldn't read or write. What was the one way God could speak to her?

Talk to God about miracles. Tell Him if you believe or don't believe in them. Ask Him to teach you the truth about them, realizing His answers don't always come instantly.

Gittyup, Dollie

Faith does nothing alone—nothing of itself,
but everything under God, by God, through God.

JOHN STOUGHTON

1. Even with Harriet's courage and knowledge of the South, she needed help from other people. Find two times in chapter six when people helped her.

_____

_____

_____

_____

Both times when Harriet was helped in this chapter, the help came at unexpected times. If you can't find them, read page 32 again.

2. God was always helping Harriet too. Write down how He helped her save her parents in this chapter.

_____

_____

STUCK? *If you can't find practical ways, look for the seemingly impossible one.*

WHAT'S THE BIBLE SAYS

Read Hebrews 11:6
Now without faith it is impossible to please God,
for the one who draws near to Him must believe
that He exists and rewards those who seek Him.

Faith means that we don't try to make it in life alone. According to this verse, whom must we depend on?

IT'S YOUR TURN

Go back and reread the It's Your Turn section in chapter two. Think about what you feared and then write down the names of one or two people who helped you through it. If no one did, write down someone you would have liked to help you.

What if these people couldn't be there? God can. Ask Him to be with you. The more you do, the more real He will become, even though you can't see Him.

CHAPTER SEVEN

A Detective Helps

The light of faith makes us see what we believe.
THOMAS AQUINAS

1. After a while people heard stories about Harriet's courage and faith. They wanted to hear more. What did Harriet end up doing in chapter seven?

_____

_____

2. What was one reason that Harriet agreed to do the above?

_____

In the 1800s when there were no TVs or movies, going to lectures was very popular, especially if the speaker was known to be a good one.

3. While Harriet did this new job, people were still helping slaves. Write down the names of two of them.

_____

_____

STUCK? *Think of barrels and wagons.*

W H A T   T H E   B I B L E   S A Y S

Read Colossians 3:16
Let the message about the Messiah dwell richly among you,
teaching and admonishing one another in all wisdom,
and singing psalms, hymns, and spiritual songs,
with gratitude in your hearts to God.

Think about this verse and what Harriet did in this chapter. What do these tell you about faith?

I T ' S   Y O U R   T U R N

We often make sharing our faith or telling people about God harder than He intended it to be. Think about Harriet. Did she know the Bible really well? What did she share?

Look back on this week and remember a way that God helped you. Share it with someone.

CHAPTER EIGHT

One Last Rescue

Faith is the pencil of the soul that pictures heavenly things.

THOMAS BURBRIDGE

1. Harriet dreamed about her people being free. When she met John Brown, she was in awe that a fine white man would share her dream. She wanted to help him, but God knew it would not be safe. How did He protect Harriet?

_____

_____

Though Joshua was the book's fictional character, I have little doubt that other people were concerned about John Brown's violence and prayed for Harriet's safety.

2. Harriet prayed that her people would one day be free. What did Harriet do that showed she had faith that God would one day grant this?

_____

_____

STUCK? *See Harriet's dream on page 41.*

W H A T   T H E   B I B L E   S A Y S

Read Hebrews 11:1, 17–31
Now faith is the reality of what is hoped for,
the proof of what is not seen.

The first verse in this passage is followed by examples of people who had faith. As you read about these people, see if you can find out what they believed in but could not see.

I T ' S   Y O U R   T U R N

Pray about understanding what faith is, even though you can't see, hear, touch, or taste it. Look up *reality* and *proof* in the dictionary. Now try rewriting the above verse.

Activities

From Slavery to Freedom with Harriet Tubman

North to Freedom

Harriet is heading north again and you're going with her!

From a slave plantation on the outskirts of **Cambridge**, Maryland, to freedom in Canada (or Canaan as the slaves call it in their songs), you'll travel on the Underground Railroad. You'll dodge danger, meet people, stop at farms, and go through cities. Often you'll walk, but some of the time you'll experience other ways that runaways traveled.

Along the journey you'll have work to do. Since you can read and write, you'll trace your route on a map. Also it's up to you to discover what last barrier must be crossed before reaching freedom.

At the bottom of each of the activities in this section, you will find a clue to help you fill in the blank spaces on the back page.

Here's help with the first one.

Clue: What was Harriet's code name?

The answer is <u>M</u> <u>O</u> <u>S</u> <u>E</u> <u>S</u>
                     13   19

Place the letter "s" in the 13th and 19th space on the last page. Each time you have a number under one of the letters in a clue, turn to the last page and put that letter in the space that has its number.

When you finish, you'll know the last barrier that the ex-slaves had to overcome to reach freedom.

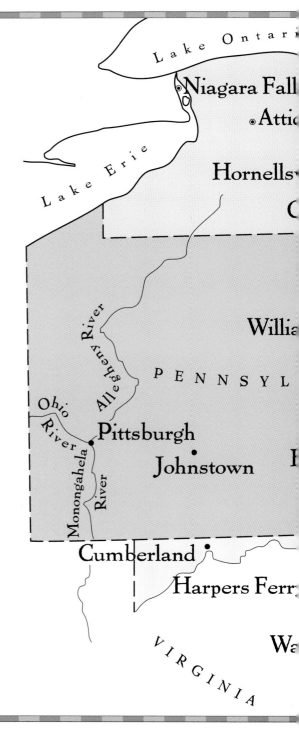

The Escape

Mapping Your Way to Freedom

Harriet did not have the advantage of a map, a compass, or road signs. Because she couldn't read, it didn't matter anyway. She had to rely on her courage, knowledge of nature, and strong faith.

But now you need to plan her route. Find her starting point, mentioned on page 63, and mark it on the map with a colored felt pen. You will discover a different town or city as you do each new activity in this section (they are marked in **bold**). Find each city's location on this map and mark it. Connect the dots as you go along with Harriet toward Canada. When you finish, you'll have one of the trails "Moses" used to take her "passengers" north.

Which way is north?
Harriet's father taught her about the stars. He, no doubt, showed her the Big Dipper and the Little Dipper. Although both of these can be in a different place in the sky depending on the time of year, one star never moves. Scientists call this star Polaris. Because it never moves, this star can be used like a compass to find north.

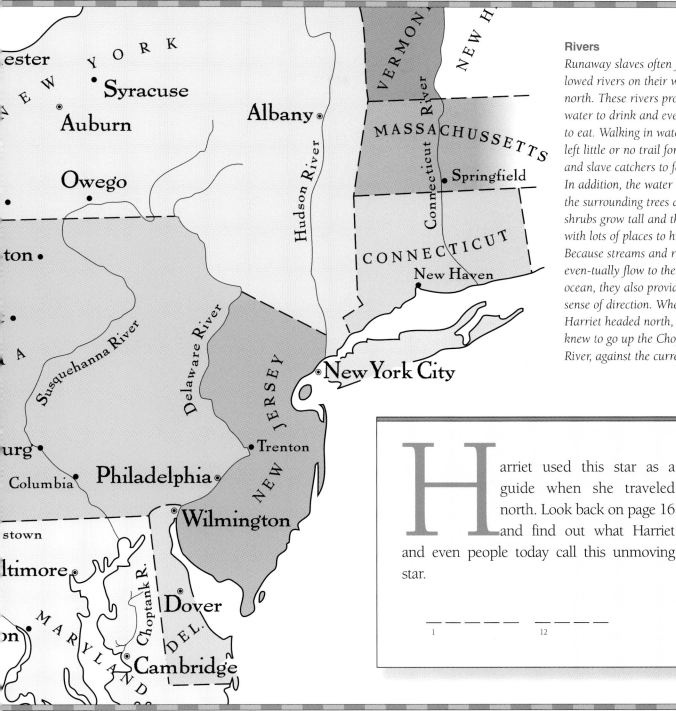

Rivers

Runaway slaves often followed rivers on their way north. These rivers provided water to drink and even fish to eat. Walking in water also left little or no trail for dogs and slave catchers to follow. In addition, the water made the surrounding trees and shrubs grow tall and thick with lots of places to hide. Because streams and rivers even-tually flow to the ocean, they also provided a sense of direction. When Harriet headed north, she knew to go up the Choptank River, against the current.

Harriet used this star as a guide when she traveled north. Look back on page 16 and find out what Harriet and even people today call this unmoving star.

— — — — —   — — — —
  1   12

Real Dangers

What You'll Face Along the Way

The first part of an escaped slave's journey brought the most danger. His or her master knew the runaway couldn't get far on foot very fast and carefully searched areas around the plantation. He used men and dogs to track the slave. If caught, the slaves were often whipped, branded, or punished in other harsh ways.

    One of the first places that you and Harriet must get past is **Dover**, Delaware. Below are some of the dangers you'll face.

Briar or Thorn Patches
When people saw a Black person with scratches and torn clothing, they suspected he or she was an escaped slave. Because runaways didn't want to be followed and caught, they often hid in large briar patches such as blackberry or wild rose thickets.

Bloodhounds

Bloodhounds have wider nostrils or nose openings than other dogs. These nostrils open to the front and down, so they pick up smells that come from the ground. Each bloodhound's nose has about 220 million cells or smell receptors that pick up scents. People have only about five million. The bloodhound picks up the smell from places where the person's feet have touched the ground or where they have brushed a rock or bush. They are gentle, friendly dogs unless they are trained to be mean.

$100 REWARD.

Ran away from my farm, near Buena Vista P. O., Prince George's County, Maryland, on the first day of April, 1855, my servant MATHEW TURNER.

He is about five feet six or eight inches high; weighs from one hundred and sixty to one hundred and eighty pounds; he is very black, and has a remarkably thick upper lip and neck; looks as if his eyes are half closed; walks slow, and talks and laughs loud.

I will give One Hundred Dollars reward to whoever will secure him in jail, so that I get him again, no matter where taken.

MARCUS DU VAL.

BUENA VISTA P. O., MD.,
MAY 10, 1855.

Reward Posters

When slaves escaped, owners printed posters describing them and sometimes even offering a reward for their return. People could often get as much as $2,000 for finding and returning a runaway slave.

Rewards for capturing "Moses" got much higher, totaling more than $40,000 because she led so many slaves to freedom. People believe Harriet Tubman led as many as three hundred slaves to freedom—that means she cost slave owners $300,000!

Slaves often traveled along rivers. When they heard the dogs approaching, they'd slip into the water so the dogs couldn't smell their scent. Look back on page 13 to find the name of the river in Maryland that Harriet followed on her way to the Underground Station at Dover, Delaware.

—— —— —— ——
16   3   6   24

The Plantation

Escaping a Cruel Life

Harriet always looked forward to her stop at **Wilmington**, Delaware. Her friend Thomas Garrett operated a station there. He helped more than two thousand escaped slaves because he knew what plantation life was like for most of them. Usually slaves worked 364 days a year with only Christmas off. Whether in the field or at the master's house, slaves worked from dawn to dusk and even longer. They got clothes only once a year and even well-treated slaves ate poor food.

Plantation Mansion
A plantation mansion often looked like a palace with verandas (porches), balconies, and winding staircases. Visitors often stayed overnight, so people had a lot of fancy bedrooms. While plantation guests slept in separate bedrooms, slave families slept together in one small room. Velvet drapes and Victorian furniture decorated plantation mansions, while a rough, handmade table was all even the luckiest of slaves had.

Cotton

Though plantations where Harriet lived in Maryland grew wheat and tobacco, the majority of slaves worked in cotton fields. Cotton grows on small trees or shrubs that form seed pods. Each pod is full of black seeds attached to fluffy white fibers that are easily spun into yarn and fabric. Cotton is strong, absorbent, and easily washed and dyed.

A Patchwork Story

People in the 1800s didn't buy blankets or comforters for their beds. They made quilts out of scraps of cloth that were left over after making clothes. The patterns on their quilts often told a story.

Pretend you are an ex-slave who wants to make a quilt that tells the story of your escape from the South and the people who helped you along the way. What are some of the pictures you would use?

One of the jobs that Harriet had to do as a slave made her very strong. Look on page 33 and find out what she chopped.

— — — — — — — — —
8   21

Slave Cabins

Slaves lived in one-room cabins. They couldn't mop their floors because they didn't have any. Slave cabins were built right on the dirt. But they did sweep the dirt. Mattresses were just big bags filled with straw or corn husks. Since they had no kitchen, slaves did all their cooking outdoors over an open fire.

QUILT FROM THE COLLECTION OF JEAN WELLS, SISTERS, OREGON.

Farm Hideouts

Where Would You Hide?

The first Northern state that Harriet came to was Pennsylvania. One of the places she usually stopped in this state was the home of William Still in **Philadelphia**. After the Fugitive Slave Law made his home unsafe, Mr. Still often sent fugitives to stay with farmers outside the city.

Farms provided a lot of places for escaping slaves to hide. They could hide in the corncrib or under a haystack. Where would you hide?

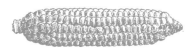

Crops

As the escaped slaves traveled north, they passed many farms. In the 1850s a farmer might grow corn, wheat, or a variety of vegetables. Some raised cows, chickens, turkeys, sheep, or hogs.

W

here was one place that Harriet hid while on a farm? Look back on page 17 for help.

__ _____ _____
5   17

Chores

In the North they didn't have slaves to work the farms. The whole family had to work hard. Children hoed corn, helped plant wheat, herded sheep, fed the hogs, milked cows, shoveled manure, churned butter, gathered eggs, and carried water. There were fences and farm buildings to build and repair and horses and wagons to take care of. Children who attended school did chores before and afterwards. They did homework late at night by lamplight.

Wheeling North

Rolling Closer to Freedom

After leaving Philadelphia, Harriet and her group headed north to **New York City**. It's 650 miles from Maryland to Canada, and runaways walked most of the way. Most people can walk three to four miles an hour on a good road. Imagine how far you could get, walking in the dead of night, without a flashlight?

On this part of Harriet's journey, she often found faster ways to travel. Here are a few of the ways in which people traveled during Harriet's day.

Wagons

A farm wagon carried hay to the barn, wood for the fireplaces, and produce to the market. It took the family to church on Sunday.

The Conestoga wagon acted as the truck or freight car of the 1800s. It was covered to protect the contents from bad weather and carried up to six tons of goods.

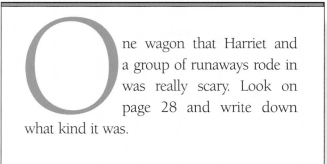

One wagon that Harriet and a group of runaways rode in was really scary. Look on page 28 and write down what kind it was.

‾‾ ‾‾   ‾‾ ‾‾ ‾‾
23   25   9   4   18

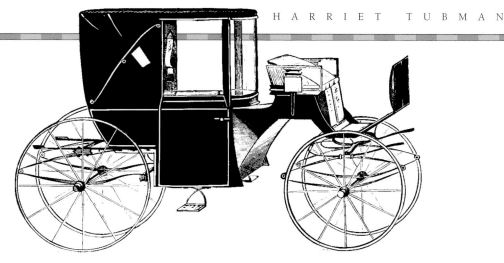

Carriages

Some people could afford a carriage for traveling. A carriage usually looked like a fancy box on wheels that was pulled by a horse. People who rode in them entered by a side door. Once inside, they were protected from bad weather. There were as many different kinds of carriages as there are different kinds of automobiles today.

Cabriolet: *A carriage with four wheels and a folding top over the back seat. It had a box for the driver to sit on in front.*

Buggy: *Light weight carriage with a folding top, which carried two people. Most popular carriage in America.*

The Railroad

Travelers in the 1850s wanted to try out the nation's newest way of traveling—the steam train! For fifty cents anyone could ride about fifteen miles. Passengers had a few complaints though. Hot ashes, blowing out of the smokestack, often burned holes in the riders' best clothes. The train also made a frightful noise, and riders always risked the danger of it getting derailed or the boiler exploding.

Going Underground

Signals, Codes, and Secrets

Any escaped slave who made it as far as **Albany**, New York, had definitely lived through some narrow escapes and had hidden in some strange places. Because slave catchers and owners searched almost everywhere, Underground Railroad agents had to think of places they wouldn't find. They also had to communicate secretly.

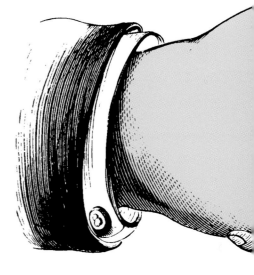

Try to Figure Out this Code:

> gniws wol, teews toirahc
>
> nimoc rof ot yrrac em emoh

Hint: The words above are spelled backwards. If you turn them around, you'll have the name of the spiritual Harriet's friends sang as she was dying.

Tunnels

Joseph Goodrich, owner of an inn in Milton, Wisconsin, dug a tunnel from his basement to a cellar in a log cabin forty feet from the house. If slave catchers came to the inn, escaping slaves, whom he let stay in his cellar, could leave through the tunnel and follow the creeks north to Canada.

Secret Handshakes

*After the Fugitive Slave Law passed, members of the
Underground Railroad could no longer safely identify themselves.
As a result, agents came up with handshakes and phrases that
would secretly reveal to other agents that they also worked in
the Underground.*

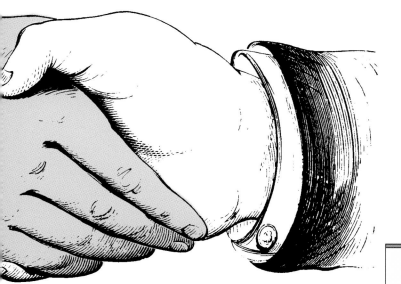

He's in the Mail

*A few slaves escaped by having someone
ship them to Philadelphia in a box or
chest. One man, later called Henry
"Box" Brown, was in a box for 26 hours.*

Signals

*Some agents in the Underground
Railroad had special signals to
warn escaping slaves not to stop
if they thought slave catchers
were watching. A lighted lantern
might signal welcome. Unlighted,
it warns blacks to pass on.*

Look in the "Did You Know" section at the
back of this book and see what code
words referred to the North Star?

— — — — —   — — — —
26   2   22   27   14

Towns & Cities

Go Around Them or Through Them?

All the way north, Harriet and her people ran into towns and cities. They had to decide whether to chance going into town or around it. **Auburn**, New York, one of Harriet Tubman's favorite stops, was much like the town pictured below.

Towns were usually built near a river. They had a village green or park in the center with a church, a general store/post office, blacksmith's shop, an inn and other businesses such as a drug store and cobblers shop.

Here are some of the things that escaped slaves might have seen as they went through Northern towns in the 1800s.

The Blacksmith

Everyone who owned a horse visited the town blacksmith. He made shoes for horses and put them on their hoofs. The blacksmith also made or repaired farm tools by heating the steel in his furnace until it could be molded into the form the farmer wanted.

Churches

People in the 1800s considered faith in God an important part of life, so towns usually built a church as one of its first buildings. Ministers and their wives frequently lived next to the church, and many gladly gave runaway slaves a place to sleep.

I f you owned a horse that needed new shoes on its hoofs, where would you take it?

___ ___ ___ ___ ___ ___ ___
10   15   20

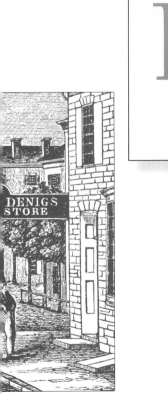

The Tailor/Seamstress

In the early 1800s, towns did not often have shops with ready-made clothes. Most people made their own cloth and sewed their own clothes, but hired tailors to do their sewing. You could have a man's shirt made for about $1.45, a pair of wool stockings cost $.50, and a wool coat cost about $5.50.

Helping Hands

People along the Way

As Harriet neared **Attica**, New York, the last stop on the Underground Railway, she felt a sense of relief — they would make it across the border and into Canada. With her relief came thanks. Many famous people, as well as not-so-famous people, had risked imprisonment and fines to help her and other runaways along the way.

Allan Pinkerton

Allan Pinkerton operated a station on the Underground Railroad near Chicago and taught escaped slaves the barrel making trade. After he started his private detective agency, his spies worked on behalf of the North. He even organized the secret service for the Union Army during the Civil War.

Susan B. Anthony

Although Susan Anthony is best known for her efforts to gain women's rights and outlaw drinking, she also was an abolitionist. She was born a Quaker and joined her family when they opened their home in Rochester, New York, to runaway slaves heading to Canada on the Underground Railroad. More than once Harriet stayed in the Anthony home.

Frederick Douglass

Frederick Douglass learned to write by tracing letters on the front of the ships where he worked as a slave in Maryland. He escaped to Massachusetts when he was about 21 years old, and he became one of the country's most outstanding speakers. He called for the slaves to be freed and used his lecture fees to help escaped slaves. During the Civil War, Frederick Douglass represented the interests of Black people to President Lincoln.

Henry David Thoreau

Henry Thoreau operated a station on the Underground Railway and lectured against slavery before it was popular to think slavery was wrong. When the town he lived in charged a tax that he thought would help slavery, he went to jail rather than pay it. In 1849 he wrote a book, Civil Disobedience, which encouraged people to refuse to obey unjust laws.

The most famous detective of the 1800s started out as a

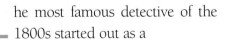

—— —— —— —— —— —— ——
 7   11   28
Go to page 84 to crack the code.

Abolitionists

This name was given to people who wanted to get rid of slavery. They first got organized in England around 1780 under a man in the British Parliament named William Wilberforce. His example, along with Quaker traditions, religious revival, and the American ideal of a "land of the free," caused many people to become abolitionists in the United States.

Anthony Burns

Though this runaway slave was recaptured in Boston and returned to his master, he eventually was sold to a friendly master. This man resold him to people in Boston who set him free and helped him go to Oberlin College. He went on to become a minister in the Canadian city of Saint Catherines.

Box Brown

The wife and children of this slave from Richmond, Virginia, were sold away from him to North Carolina. Determined to escape, he asked a white friend to help him build a wooden crate lined with coarse wool. The friend nailed the crate shut with Brown inside. He then mailed it to Philadelphia. For twenty-six hours he traveled north as cargo, often on his head. But he made it safely!

Bucktown, Maryland

This plantation slave town got its name from the term owners used when referring to young, male slaves—bucks. It no longer exists today.

Canada

By 1826 there were so many runaways living in Canada that Southern slave owners asked Congress to work out a treaty for returning slaves. It took a year and two requests before Canada sent this reply: "It is utterly impossible to agree to a stipulation for the surrender of fugitive slaves." By 1852 about twenty-five thousand runaways lived in our neighboring country.

Christmas for Slaves

Since this was one of the few times slaves didn't have to work, they usually held a big celebration. In the daylight hours of the holiday, men and women often quilted, using dyed flour sacks and scraps of fabric. Then they put together a big feast with the extra food rations that were usually given for the occasion. Next came singing and dancing, sometimes accompanied by fiddles made from gourds with horsehair strings. Usually the party lasted until dawn.

William Lloyd Garrison

Declaration of Independence and Slavery

When Thomas Jefferson wrote the first draft of the Declaration of Independence, he included a strong attack against slavery. Congress removed it except for these words: "We hold these Truths to be self-evident, that all Men are created equal, that they are endowed by their Creator with certain unalienable Rights, that among these are Life, Liberty, and the pursuit of Happiness."

A slave plays on a homemade instrument

Did you

Freedom Park

In 1944, the city of Auburn, New York, dedicated this park to the memory of Harriet Tubman. It is on North Seventeenth Street.

Frederick Douglass

This famous Black speaker and abolitionist was born a slave named Frederick Augustus Washington Bailey. It took him two years and two tries before escaping in 1838 to Massachusetts, where he changed his last name to Douglass. Before dying in 1895, he became the US marshal for the District of Columbia and the US minister to Haiti.

Garrison's Near Lynching

While he lived in Boston, William Lloyd Garrison in 1831 started publishing an abolitionist newspaper called the Liberator. By 1835 it had upset a lot of people. On October 21 a mob of two thousand well-dressed, respectable men turned out, bent on hanging Garrison. The mayor and police got Garrison away but locked him in the jail for safety. Garrison wrote on the wall of his jail cell that the mob wanted to kill him for "preaching the abominable [hateful] and dangerous doctrine that all men are created equal and that all oppression is odious [sickening] in the sight of God."

Harriet's Home

After her parents died, Harriet lived in the house she had bought for them. In 1903 she turned it over to the African Methodist Episcopal Zion Church to be used as a home for the sick, the poor, and the homeless. She lived there until her death in 1913. Today her home has been restored to it's original appearance.

exist today, we know that she went south at least eighteen times and set free around three hundred slaves. Slaveholders were so troubled by "Moses" that by the time the Civil War broke out, the reward for her was up to six thousand dollars!

Henry David Thoreau

This member of the Underground became a famous American writer. While sheltering runaways in his home in Concord, Massachusetts, he wrote two of his best-known works, *Life in the Woods* and *Civil Disobedience*.

Nat Turner

In 1831 this popular slave led a violent rebellion in Virginia. He believed he'd been chosen by God to lead his people to freedom. Many masters and their families were killed during the revolt. State militiamen and volunteers stopped the rebellion and hanged an unknown number of slaves. As a result of this rebellion, restrictions were put on the movements of slaves, and Turner's song of deliverance, "Go Down, Moses," was forbidden. The violence of this revolt ended all abolitionist sympathies in the south.

North Star

Many slaves like Harriet made their way to freedom by following the North Star at night. Also known as Polaris, the North Star is part of a constellation the slaves nicknamed the "Drinking Gourd"; today we call it the Little Dipper. If clouds covered the stars at night, some slaves stayed hidden until the sky cleared. During the day, runaways had to use other methods to tell which way was north. They looked for moss on trees, believing that it only grew on the north side of the trunk. Also the slave could follow the direction of a river.

Pinkerton Detective Agency

What made a barrel-maker-turned-sheriff think of starting a detective agency in 1850? Undoubtedly the answer lies in both fiction and fact. From 1841 to 1845 Edgar Allan Poe brought to life the first fictional detective, C. Auguste Dupin. He used deduction to solve "The Murders in the Rue Morgue," "The Mystery of Marie Roget," and

four other fictional cases. Meanwhile the first real-life detective was solving murders in Paris. Francois Vidocq was head of the Criminal Investigation Department in France. Between these real and fictitious detectives, Allan Pinkerton could easily have gotten his idea for starting a detective agency.

Abraham Lincoln campaigns against slavery

Political Freedom

Black people were not given the right to vote in United States elections until the Fifteenth Amendment to the Constitution was ratified in 1870. And even after gaining this right, poll taxes continued to keep Blacks from voting until 1964, when the Twenty-fourth Amendment made poll taxes illegal. But even before Blacks had the right to vote, educator and diplomat John Mercer Langston was elected town clerk of Brownhelm, Ohio. He was the first Black man to win an elected office in the United States.

Everything You Ever Wanted to Know about the Underground Railroad

know?

Harriet's Parents

Harriet Green and Benjamin Ross, Harriet Tubman's parents, were second-generation slaves owned by Edward Brodess. Their grandparents came from the Ashanti tribe in today's central Ghana, a country in Africa; they were abducted from their African home and sold into slavery in 1725.

Harriet's Rescues

No one knows exactly how many trips Harriet made back into the South or how many slaves she rescued. But from the few records that

Lincoln-Douglas Debates

By the time Abraham Lincoln and Stephen Douglas held these seven debates in 1858 during their Illinois campaign for United States senator, the issue of slavery was dividing the country. The Kansas-Nebraska Act, sponsored by Douglas, angered many Northerners. Lincoln attacked slavery but not slaveholders. In the end Douglas won the senate seat, but two years later he lost the presidential election to Lincoln.

Ralph Waldo Emerson

Ralph Waldo Emerson

This noted American writer got involved in the abolition movement and frequently gave lectures against it. In one speech to the Anti-Slavery Society of New York, he proposed that slavery could be ended by offering to pay slaveholders for their slaves. His estimated cost was two hundred million dollars!

Rewards

A reward was not offered for every slave who ran away. Many had posters with only their description on them, not an offer of money for their capture and return. But slaves who were worth a lot of money, such as young and healthy or trained ones, often had a price put on their heads. It would cost an owner up to $1,000 to buy another slave to take the runaway's place, so a reward was often cheaper.

Secret Handshakes

George De Baptiste and William Lambert, Underground Railroad agents in Michigan, wanted to develop a secret system of signs to help agents identify each other. They created the Order of African-American Mysteries. Members used secret handshakes, passwords, and other signals that came to be used throughout the Underground system.

Sarah Bradford

This schoolteacher admired Harriet Tubman and became her friend. When she saw Harriet's problem of trying to pay for her home, Sarah decided to do something to raise money for her friend; she wrote Harriet's life story. Harriet got twelve hundred dollars from the sale of Sarah's book and was able to pay off the loan on her home. Seventeen years later, Sarah wrote another book to help her friend. Without these "as-told-to" biographies, we would know little about Harriet Tubman today.

Uncle Tom's Cabin
by Harriet Beecher Stowe

Shackles

Shackles are made of iron and have been around since ancient times. They have two thick rings that are connected by a chain. Placed on wrists and ankles, they were used to keep a person captive. The heavy iron caused sores and cuts with little hope of healing until the shackles came off. Slaves often wore them on the ships bringing them over from Africa. Once on plantations, many wore them when being punished.

The Colt revolver was invented in 1836 by Samuel Colt.

Slave Ships

The condition of these ships and the treatment of slaves on them is unthinkable today. Confined to the dark cargo hold in the bottom of the ship, slaves were crowded in with no beds or bathrooms. Exposed to heat, cold, and common sickness with little food or water, many slaves died before they ever reached America. If the ship ran into trouble and sank, the iron shackles on the slaves dragged them under and they drowned.

Slaver

John Newton was a "slaver," a man who picked up human cargo along

the coast of Africa and shipped it to the Americas in the 1700s. For years he made lots of money in the slave trade, but then he turned to God. His new faith led him to men like William Wilberforce, who convinced him that slavery was wrong. John left the slave trade and later wrote the famous hymn, "Amazing Grace." Its first words are, "Amazing grace! How sweet the sound that saved a wretch like me."

Spirituals

Spirituals were first sung in Christian revival meetings. As slaves heard and adopted them, they added music traditions from their native land of Africa. Some of these additions included finger-snapping, clapping, stamping, and an excited dance called "ring-shout." Usually one slave sang and then the group responded in chorus to the words. This kind of singing is usually referred to as call and response. Many of the African music traditions used in spirituals were later used by rock-n-roll singers.

Hauling bales of cotton to market

Still Day
William Still's slave parents, Levin and Charity, started a family that has, over time, included doctors, teachers, scientists, and military heroes. Descendants continue to have reunions, called Still Days. In 1983 more than a hundred family members celebrated their 114th reunion in Lawnside, New Jersey!

Suspension Bridge
The bridge over Niagara Falls that Harriet and her "passengers" crossed was only planks laced together by rope. Today the well-engineered Whirlpool Bridge has replaced the rickety wooden one.

Tobacco
Tobacco comes from the big leaves of a plant that grows three to ten feet tall. It originally came from the Americas but explorers took it back to Europe after seeing natives smoke it. Christopher Columbus smoked the dried leaves through a tube called a tobago, and soon people began to call the plant "tobacco." In Harriet's day most tobacco was grown south of her plantation in Virginia, Kentucky, and Tennessee. Today China is the largest grower of tobacco, while the US is second.

Two Worlds
While Harriet ran rescue trips and the Underground Railroad grew, our country made other changes: the *New York Times* newspaper got started, the first baseball teams played competitive games, Samuel Colt invented the Colt revolver, John Augustus Sutter found gold in California, Henry Steinway started a piano manufacturing business, and Gail Borden marketed condensed milk.

Thomas Garrett
This well-known agent for the Underground Railroad had all of his property sold at public auctions in order to pay fines for breaking the law by giving food and shelter to runaway slaves. The fines did not stop him. During the operation of the Underground, twenty-five hundred fugitive slaves passed through his home in Wilmington, Maryland.

Harriet Beecher Stowe

Uncle Tom's Cabin
When Harriet Beecher Stowe started writing this famous novel, she thought it would be a short story. It ended up a novel that sold three hundred thousand copies the first year after it was published. Theaters immediately started producing plays starring Uncle Tom. Many readers and play-goers who enjoyed this moving fictional story turned against slavery after learning the story of Uncle Tom, a kindly, old slave. Though first owned by a good man, financial trouble caused the owner to sell Tom. He promised to find him and buy him back as soon as possible, but Tom's new owner had a cruel overseer named Simon Legree. The story goes on to expose, in graphic detail, the cruel things Tom saw and the beating that led to his death.

Tobacco plant grown by many Southern plantations

Underground Railroad
It went by many names, including the Trackless Train, the Emancipation Car, and the Mysterious Track. Many believe its most-used name came from a comment made by a slave owner who couldn't find his escaped slave: "It's as if he has gone off on some underground road."

A runaway slave stops for a rest on her way to freedom.

Today in Ashtabula, Ohio, the descendant of a strong abolitionist, Tim Hubbard, helps conduct an Underground Railroad pilgrimage every year. He and those who accompany him retrace a Northern route from West Virginia to Ashtabula, where ship captains took runaways across Lake Erie into Canada.

Freedom at Last!

In this book, there are numbers underneath some of the letters in the blanks you filled in. Match those letters up with the numbered spaces below, and you will discover the last obstacle you must cross before getting into Canada.

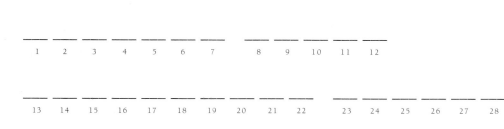

___ ___ ___ ___ ___ ___ ___   ___ ___ ___ ___ ___
1   2   3   4   5   6   7   8   9   10 11 12

___ ___ ___ ___ ___ ___ ___ ___ ___ ___   ___ ___ ___ ___ ___ ___
13 14 15 16 17 18 19 20 21 22   23 24 25 26 27 28

Congratulations you have made it to **Niagara Falls** and into Canada. You are safe, at last!

Enclosed in your kit is a reproduction of the "certificate of freedom" issued to a slave named John Jones proving that he could no longer be owned as a slave and insuring his Freedom.

Answer to the last obstacle: *Niagara Falls Suspension Bridge.*

Answers to clues: *Moses, North Star, Choptank River, Firewood, Potato Hole, Brick Wagon, Drinking Gourd, Blacksmith, Barrel Maker.*